SWAGGER WARS III ™

THE MASK SOCIETY ™

They liked our confidence -

until we took off the masks.

AUTHOR - JOYCE LEE

ISBN Hardback: 979-8-9930206-5-5

Library of Congress Control Number: 2025922617

Text copyright 2025 by Joyce Lee

Illustration copyright 2025 by Umair Ali

Swagger Wars III ™ *The Mask Society*™ and the tagline *Unmask Your Power*™ are trademarks of **Spirit, Inc.**, a 501(c)(3) nonprofit organization based in Texas.

Published by **Spirit, Inc.**

Houston, Texas | www.spirit-np.infowCover and Interior Design by Umair Ali

First Edition – 2025

Printed in the United States of America

10 9 8 7 6 5 4 3 2 1

Dedication

To the unshakable, the unfiltered, the unafraid.

You are the reason masks crack and change begins.

Unmask Your Power

by Joyce Lee

They told us to smile wide,
to keep our edges smooth,
to fit the frame,
to shrink the truth.

We learned to sparkle on cue,
hide cracks with filters and flair,
but silence cuts deeper
when no one knows you're there.

Swagger, they said, is showtime —
the walk, the fit, the fame.
But we found our swagger
when we stopped playing the game.

Power isn't perfect posture,
or noise made to impress.
It's whispering, "I'm still here,"
when your world's a mess.

So take off the mask —
the one they told you to wear.
Let your scars see daylight,
let your truth fill the air.

Because confidence isn't costume,
and courage isn't choreographed.
It's the sound of your own voice
echoing back — unmasked.

CONTENTS

WHY I WROTE SWAGGER WARS III™
THE MASK SOCIETY™

Every day, young people walk into schools carrying invisible burdens. They smile when they're hurting, act confident when they're scared, and wear masks just to survive the social pressure around them. *Swagger Wars III: The Mask Society*™ was born from that truth — the kind we don't always talk about, but we all recognize.

Middle and high school students live through more than academics. They navigate self-image, bullying, shame, comparison, and identity. They want to belong, but they also want to be seen for who they really are. This story pulls the mask off — literally and emotionally — to show what happens when students find the courage to be authentic in a world that rewards performance over honesty.

As the founder of Spirit, Inc., I've met hundreds of students who've struggled with hygiene poverty, social judgment, and the quiet loss of confidence that follows. *The Mask Society*™ represents them — every student who has ever felt unseen, unheard, or unworthy because they couldn't meet someone else's definition of "enough."

This book isn't just a story. It's a mirror — a reminder that confidence without authenticity is just another disguise. True confidence begins when we stop hiding and start healing.

My hope is that readers, whether middle schoolers or young adults, see themselves somewhere in these pages — and realize that taking off the mask isn't weakness. It's power.

— Joyce Lee

Founder & President, *Spirit, Inc.*

Author, *The Swagger Wars*™ *Trilogy*

THE MASK AND THE MIRROR

They say the mirror never lies.

But sometimes, it doesn't tell the whole truth either.

When Nyla James looked into the bathroom mirror that morning, she didn't see a girl starting over.

She saw a performance waiting for its cue.

The hoodie was clean, the shoes scuffed but solid. Her hair was tied back, not because she wanted it that way, but because confidence — the kind other people noticed — was supposed to look effortless.

She took a deep breath, wiped the fog from the glass, and whispered to her reflection,

"You got this."

The girl in the mirror didn't answer. She just stared back, uncertain but brave enough to keep pretending.

For years, Nyla had learned that pretending was survival.

At her old school, confidence wasn't a feeling — it was armor. If you laughed loud enough, dressed bold enough, or walked like you belonged, people stopped asking questions about what you didn't have.

And what Nyla didn't have — what no one talked about — was simple: safety in being seen.

That's what made Riverstone High different.

It was new, big, glossy — a place where everything shined a little too perfectly.

And perfect, she knew, was the most dangerous mask of all.

On the bus ride that morning, she sketched what she couldn't say.

A blank face with cracks spreading from the corners of its smile.

Underneath, she wrote one word in red ink: **Truth.**

It wasn't art, exactly. It was a question — one she hadn't found the courage to ask out loud:

What happens when the mask starts to break?

She closed the notebook and looked out the window.

Students stood in clusters outside the school entrance, laughing, posing, snapping photos.

Every laugh sounded rehearsed. Every photo looked like proof of something they didn't really feel.

The world didn't need more masks. It needed mirrors.

But no one tells you how heavy mirrors can be when you're the one holding them.

That night before her first day, her mom had said something Nyla couldn't stop replaying:

"The world's gonna try to teach you what to wear, how to talk, what to hide.

But don't let it tell you who you are, baby.

Just remember — swagger isn't what you show them.

It's what survives when everything else falls away."

At the time, it sounded like one of those grown-up phrases that belonged in a frame.

Now, standing in front of Riverstone's glass doors, it felt like the only truth she had left.

The hallway smelled like lemon polish and ambition.

Posters lined the walls: *Be Bold. Be Beautiful. Be the Brand.*

A girl with glossy braids and a photo-ready smile handed out flyers that said "JOIN THE SWAGGER STANDARD — CONFIDENCE IS OUR CODE."

Nyla took one, not because she believed it, but because she wanted to understand the world she'd just entered.

Confidence is our code.

The words sat in her palm like a dare.

She didn't know yet that those same words would break the school in half — that they'd spark a movement, a controversy, a choice that would make Riverstone famous for all the right and wrong reasons.

For now, she only knew one thing:

If truth was a mirror, this school had forgotten how to look.

That night, she would draw again — a face behind a mask, a crowd in the background, and one phrase etched beneath the sketch in bold letters:

Unmask Your Power.

It would start as a whisper.

A drawing on a page.

A secret shared between courage and fear.

And from there, the ripple would begin.

Unmask Your Power.

CHAPTER ONE:

THE CAFETERIA CODE

The first thing Nyla James noticed about Riverstone High wasn't how big it was.

It was how polished everything felt — like the school had been scrubbed for a photoshoot and the students knew they were the stars.

By the time she found the cafeteria, her nerves buzzed from too many stares. The room glittered with noise — sneakers squeaking, trays clattering, laughter that sounded more rehearsed than real. Tables weren't just for eating; they were stages.

There was a *sports table*, a *fashion table*, an *arts table* that looked like a mood board, and in the middle — the *Swagger Circle* — where the most confident people on campus sat.

At least, they looked confident.

Nyla paused at the end of the line, clutching her lunch tray. Her jeans were clean but faded. Her hoodie had a small bleach spot on the sleeve. She could already feel the contrast between her thrift store survival and everyone else's curated perfection.

She exhaled quietly. *You don't need new. You just need purpose.* Her mother's words again. She straightened her back and scanned for a seat.

"New face alert," someone said behind her.

Nyla turned to see a girl with honey-colored braids and a badge that read **Liana**

Cruz — Student Body President.

Her smile was camera-ready, the kind that could win awards and elections.

"You're the transfer from Northside, right?" Liana said, sliding her tray next to Nyla's.

"Yeah."

"I'm Liana. I run student council and the *Swagger Standard* committee."

"The what?"

Liana laughed like she'd heard that question a hundred times. "It's our confidence initiative. Teaches leadership, image, and presence. You'll love it."

Before Nyla could respond, a shout rose from the center of the cafeteria. A group of football players had gathered around a table where one of them stood — tall, broad-shouldered, and impossible to ignore. His varsity jacket hung open, revealing a white tee and the kind of easy posture that came from knowing you ruled the room.

"That's **Dre Vega**," Liana said with a small sigh. "Quarterback. School celebrity. Rebel without a clue."

At that moment, Dre was performing a mock introduction of the "Swagger Standard" pledge.

He put one hand to his heart, voice booming:

"I solemnly swear to look flawless, act fearless, and never, ever let the cafeteria see me sweat!"

The table exploded in laughter. Even a few teachers smiled and shook their heads.

"Ridiculous," Liana muttered. "He thinks everything's a joke."

But Nyla saw something else. When the laughter faded, Dre's smile dropped for a fraction of a second — like he was exhausted from being the person everyone expected him to be.

Liana snapped her fingers in front of Nyla. "Earth to new girl. Ignore him. Come sit with us."

Nyla followed, sliding into an open seat beside Liana's polished group. Their trays looked like restaurant menus — salads with extras, designer water bottles, coordinated color schemes. They smiled politely but didn't speak. Phones glowed under the table; everyone seemed to be half in another world.

"Riverstone runs on confidence," Liana said. "That's our motto. Presentation matters here. People judge — so we lead."

Nyla nodded, though her stomach twisted. She picked at her sandwich.

Across the cafeteria, Dre's crew was recording something on a phone. "We're doing a 'Swagger Check,'" one of them yelled — scanning tables for outfits, laughter loud enough to echo.

When they reached Nyla's side, she could feel her pulse climb. The camera panned past designer sneakers, fresh braids, luxury bags… then stopped on her thrift hoodie and frayed backpack strap.

"Hold up," someone said. "We got a *budget baddie* in the house!"

The table snickered.

Nyla froze. The room blurred into heat and noise. She wasn't sure what hurt more — the insult or the fact that no one at Liana's table said anything.

Before she could speak, Dre appeared — tossing his teammates a sharp look. "Cut it out."

The laughter stopped instantly.

Dre turned to Nyla, his voice lower, genuine. "Don't mind them. They act dumb for clicks."

She met his eyes. There was something there — a flicker of shame maybe, or recognition.

"I'm fine," she said quietly.

But she wasn't.

As Dre walked off, Nyla noticed he didn't laugh with the group. He just shoved his phone into his pocket and left through the side door, the noise swallowing him again.

Liana leaned in. "You'll learn fast. Around here, image is everything. Even when you're right."

That afternoon, Nyla found an empty seat near the cafeteria's far window. The laughter, the stares, the silence — it all churned in her chest. She pulled her sketchbook from her bag and started to draw.

The first lines came shaky, then sharper: a face behind a cracked mask, one eye crying, the other smiling.

When she finished, she scrawled across the top in red pen:

Who are we when no one's watching?

A shadow crossed her page.

"That's cold," a voice said.

She looked up. Dre stood there again, tray in hand. No teammates this time. Just him.

"It's real," he added. "No one draws real anymore."

"Thanks."

He hesitated, glancing at the sketch again. "You ever feel like people here are just… performing?"

"All the time," Nyla said.

Dre chuckled. "You'll fit right in, then. We could use someone who remembers what being real looks like."

Before she could reply, he was gone — swallowed back into the blur of noise and reputation.

After school, Nyla sat on her bed, replaying the day.

Every smile at Riverstone felt polished. Every compliment sounded like a contract. And Dre Vega — the most confident person in the room — looked like he wanted to disappear behind his own swagger.

She opened her sketchbook again. The cracked mask stared up at her.

Underneath it, she wrote four words that felt like a whisper to herself:

Unmask Your Power.

The words pulsed on the page — quiet, dangerous, true.

CHAPTER TWO:
THE POST

By Friday morning, Nyla's drawing had taken on a life of its own.

She hadn't meant for anyone to see it. It was supposed to stay in her sketchbook — private, personal, unfinished. But sometime between fifth period Thursday and the first bell Friday, someone had taken a picture of it and posted it online.

Now, her cracked mask sketch — the one with the words **"Who are we when no one's watching?"** — was everywhere.

Screens glowed with it in the hallway. Someone had even printed copies and taped them on lockers. A caption floated beneath it on the school's social feed:

"Anonymous art found in the cafeteria. Deep or depressing? #RiverstoneRealTalk"

By lunch, the post had more comments than the football team's highlight reel.

When Nyla stepped into the cafeteria, the buzz hit her like static.

"Yo, that's her," someone whispered.

"The art girl."

"She's the one who drew the mask thing!"

She felt her cheeks heat, wishing she could sink into the floor.

At her old school, nobody cared about her drawings. Here, they were headline material.

As she stood frozen by the door, Liana Cruz approached, flanked by two student council reps with tablets in hand.

"Nyla!" Liana's smile was bright enough to blind. "Can we talk?"

Nyla blinked. "Uh… sure?"

Liana linked her arm through Nyla's like they'd been friends forever. "This whole thing you started — it's getting traction. People are responding to it. We're thinking about featuring your art on the *Swagger Standard* page."

"The what?"

Liana's tone shifted slightly — still sweet, but firmer. "The school's official confidence campaign. We highlight positive student messages. You could be our next feature if we add a slogan — something uplifting."

Nyla frowned. "It wasn't meant to be… branding. It was a question."

Liana's smile didn't falter. "Everything's branding here, Nyla. You'll get used to it."

She gave a small wave and glided off, her entourage trailing behind.

Across the cafeteria, Dre Vega watched the whole thing.

He sat at the football table, his teammates loud and careless, throwing fries and recording each other for their Friday "Swagger Snap." But Dre wasn't laughing.

He recognized the drawing — he'd seen Nyla make it. Something about it had stuck with him. The cracked mask looked too much like his life.

Every Friday, he put on his version of it — quarterback grin, perfect walk, perfect girl, perfect leadership. Coaches called him *the face of Riverstone.*

But he didn't feel like a face anymore. Just the mask holding one together.

Now everyone was talking about Nyla's art like it was a rebellion.

"Yo, Dre," his teammate Marcus said, nudging him. "That drawing's lowkey fire. You think she meant it about this school?"

Dre's jaw tightened. "She meant it about everybody."

Marcus laughed. "Man, you're deep today."

But Dre wasn't joking.

When the lunch bell rang, Nyla escaped outside to the bleachers behind the gym. She needed quiet — air that didn't sound like opinions.

She opened her sketchbook again, flipping past the original drawing to a new blank page.

She wanted to draw something else, but all she could think about were the comments.

Some were kind — *This is so real!* — but others stung: *Whoever drew this just wants attention.*

Another pity artist.

Maybe she should smile more.

She sighed.

A shadow stretched across her page.

"You really caused a scene," Dre said, walking up with his duffel slung over his shoulder.

"Yeah," she muttered. "By accident."

"You know what's crazy?" he said, sitting beside her. "People can't stop talking about it, but no one's really listening. They're too busy arguing whether it's deep or depressing."

Nyla smirked. "Typical."

Dre nodded slowly. "You asked a real question. This school hates real questions."

He looked out at the empty field, voice quieter. "You ever feel like people only like the idea of you? Not you?"

"All the time."

They sat in silence for a while, wind tugging at the edge of Nyla's hoodie.

Then Dre said, "I think what you drew scares people. 'Cause once you start asking who's real, half of Riverstone disappears."

Nyla looked at him curiously. "Including you?"

He smiled, but it didn't reach his eyes. "Maybe especially me."

That afternoon, the school's social media page dropped a post:

The Swagger Standard presents: #UnmaskConfidence — Art by Riverstone's own Nyla James!

"Confidence means showing your best self!"

Underneath was Nyla's drawing — but edited.

The cracked lines were smoothed over. The words *"Who are we when no one's watching?"* were gone.

In their place: *"Be flawless. Be fearless. Be you!"*

Nyla stared at the screen, disbelief turning to anger.

They'd stolen her truth and turned it into propaganda.

By Monday morning, her stomach hurt walking through the halls. Posters of her *"new and improved"* drawing lined the walls.

She tore one down, shoving it into her backpack.

That's when TJ caught up with her — hoodie up, earbuds in, a recorder hanging around his neck.

"You saw it too, huh?" he said. "They sanitized your message. Classic Riverstone PR."

She nodded. "I didn't give them permission."

TJ grinned slightly. "Then maybe it's time to take your message back."

"How?"

"Underground," he said simply. "My podcast. *Unfiltered.* We drop truth anonymously. Let people hear what the Standard won't post."

Nyla hesitated. "You think anyone will care?"

"They already do," TJ said. "They just don't know it yet."

That night, she and TJ sat in her small apartment kitchen, recording quietly while her mom graded papers in the other room.

"This is *Unfiltered*," TJ said into the mic, voice steady. "Today's topic: The Mask."

Nyla's hands trembled slightly. "We wear them every day," she began. "The confidence mask, the happy mask, the 'I'm fine' mask. But what if taking it off doesn't make you weak? What if that's the bravest thing you can do?"

Her voice cracked on the last sentence — not from fear, but from truth.

TJ cut the mic. "That was perfect," he said softly.

They posted the clip anonymously under the tag **#UnmaskYourPower**.

By morning, it had 3,000 views.

The next day, the cafeteria felt different. Whispering replaced laughter. Posters were torn down, replaced by hand-drawn masks and scribbled phrases:

"Be real."

"Swagger isn't silence."

"#UnmaskYourPower."

Liana Cruz looked furious as she stormed into the principal's office. Dre watched from the hallway, quietly smiling for the first time in months.

When Nyla walked in later, students nodded at her — small acknowledgments, quiet thanks.

No one said the words out loud yet, but she could feel it.

Something had started.

Something that didn't belong to the school — or the Standard — anymore.

It belonged to them.

That night, Nyla opened her sketchbook again.

This time she drew three faces side by side — hers, TJ's, and Dre's — half masked, half bare, each with cracks like light beams instead of wounds.

Beneath it, she wrote:

The Mask Society.

She didn't plan the name.

It just felt right — like the next step in a story she didn't mean to start, but couldn't stop now.

CHAPTER THREE:

THE BACKLASH

By Wednesday, the posters were gone.

Custodians moved down the corridors like a slow tide, peeling off every hand-drawn mask and every scribbled **#UnmaskYourPower** with gloved fingers and citrus spray. The hallway that had felt newly alive on Tuesday returned to its clean, echoing shine. Riverstone High, restored.

Then the principal's voice came over the intercom.

"Good morning, Riverstone. A reminder that all school communications must be approved by administration. Unauthorized messaging, recordings, or postings using the Riverstone name violate policy. Students who disrupt the learning environment will face consequences under the Code of Conduct. Thank you."

The speaker clicked off. Conversations thinned to threads.

Nyla felt the room's temperature drop even though the air didn't move. Across the cafeteria, Liana stood with a clipboard and a tight smile, conferring with two assistant principals like a publicist after a scandal. TJ slid into the seat across from Nyla and set down a bag of vending-machine pretzels like it was contraband.

"Morning to you too," he said, voice low. "Guess freedom of speech took a personal day."

Nyla stared at the blank wall where one of her favorite drawings had been twenty minutes earlier. "They cleaned the cracks out of the mirrors," she said. "Now everyone can pretend again."

TJ cracked a pretzel stick. "They can try."

At the football table, Dre watched the same scene unfold from a different angle. His teammates were louder than usual, as if volume could keep reality back.

"You see the admin blast?" Marcus asked, thumping a Gatorade on the table. "They're coming for the mask kids. Good. School was getting weird."

"Because people were honest for five minutes?" Dre said.

Marcus snorted. "Because we play Friday. Distractions are how you lose."

"Sometimes distractions are the reason you win," Dre said, surprising himself. "Sometimes you stop pretending, and the weight lifts."

Several helmets turned.

"Bro," said Jamal, a lineman with a permanent grin, "you recording poetry now? Chill."

Laughter spilled and then stopped when Coach Ruiz stepped through the door. The team rose like a single body. Coach didn't smile. He never did on game week.

"Practice. Now," he said. Then, after the others moved, he put a hand on Dre's shoulder. "Quarterback with me."

They walked the long hallway past trophy cases full of shining faces. Coach didn't speak until they were inside his office, door shut, the hum of the vending machine filling the space between sentences.

"You've seen the noise," Coach said.

"Yes, sir."

"I've also seen your name in three rumors and your face in two videos."

Dre swallowed. "I didn't post anything."

"I didn't say you did." Coach sat. "I'm saying this team needs a leader who can walk into a stadium and not bring the internet with him."

Dre met his eyes. "What if the leader this team needs is a person and not a brand?"

Coach's jaw flexed. For a second he looked almost proud. Then the mask of professional concern slid back. "On Friday, be a quarterback. You want to save the world, do it Saturday."

"Sir—"

"Vega." Coach's voice was a warning now. "Your job is to keep the huddle together. You can't do that looking over the stands for a cause."

Dre stood there, heartbeat loud in his ears, and realized he was no longer sure the huddle was the thing worth holding together.

"Yes, sir," he said anyway.

During third period, two assistant principals visited art class. They spoke to Ms. Calderon in the doorway, faces arranged in gentle concern, then turned to the room.

"We've had reports of unapproved posters and anonymous recordings," one said. "If anyone has information about where these messages are originating, please share it. We want our school to be positive and safe."

Safe.

Nyla's pencil slowed. The word slid through her like a cold hand.

After they left, Ms. Calderon moved around the room adjusting paint trays. She paused by Nyla's desk, a question in her eyes she didn't ask. Instead she whispered, "Truth has a way of surviving bleach," and kept walking.

By last bell, the day felt like a held breath. Students avoided eye contact, phones stayed face-down. Liana's official *Swagger Standard* account posted a carousel of "approved confidence steps." Step 1: Smile. Step 2: Stand tall. Step 3: Be fearless.

Nyla read it twice and wasn't sure whether to cry or laugh.

Her phone buzzed. A text from TJ: **Art room. Back stairwell. 4:10. Bring the sketchbook.**

She took the long way, past the lockers that still smelled faintly of citrus and loss. The back stairwell always ran cooler. She opened the art-room door and found the lights off, the room golden with late sun.

TJ leaned against a cabinet labeled *Ceramics—Do Not Move*. Dre stood near the drying racks, helmet under his arm like he wasn't sure yet if he had the right to put it down.

Nyla blinked. "You came."

Dre nodded. "I'm tired of hearing my own voice say the wrong things."

They stood awkwardly for a second, three islands deciding whether to be a shore. Then TJ lifted his recorder and set it on the table, unthreatening and still.

"So," he said. "We can complain. Or we can organize."

"Organize what?" Nyla asked.

Dre set the helmet on a stool and rolled his shoulders like he was shedding twenty pounds of expectation. "A team that doesn't need a field."

TJ grinned. "I like him."

Nyla opened her sketchbook. On the newest page, three faces—hers, TJ's, Dre's—looked back at them, half masked, half bright. Beneath them, in red ink: **The Mask Society.**

Her cheeks warmed. "I… wrote the words last night. It just appeared."

"Names matter," TJ said softly, like a vow.

Dre sat. "If we're doing this, we do it right. No messy drama. No clout chasing. Rules."

"Rules?" Nyla said, surprised and a little relieved.

"Yeah," Dre said. "I've lived in locker rooms since I was six. People don't change without a code."

He took a marker from a jar, found an empty newsprint pad, and wrote **The Mask Society — Code** in block letters.

"Rule One," he said. "Consent. No story is ours to tell unless the person wants it told."

TJ nodded. "Rule Two: Anonymity by default. If someone wants their name attached, that's their choice. Otherwise we protect them."

Nyla thought of the posters being peeled down. "Rule Three: Proof. We don't post rumors. We share truths that help, not hurt."

"Rule Four," TJ added, warming now, "No shaming. No punching down. Our job is to unmask lies, not people."

They looked to Nyla. She tapped the pen against the table, thinking about the way the cafeteria had gone quiet at the intercom, about Ms. Calderon's whisper, about her mom's red ribbon tied on a zipper pull for courage.

"Rule Five," she said. "Care. If we crack something open, we stay. We connect people to help. We don't walk away."

Silence sat with them for a moment, not heavy, just full. The kind of silence that meant a real thing had been named.

TJ drew a box on the newsprint. "Okay. Actions."

Nyla raised a hand like they were in class. "A story wall," she said. "Not on the main hallway—too obvious. In the old auditorium lobby no one uses. Big sheets of butcher paper with 'What mask do you wear?' Students can add notes. We change the paper every day so they can't erase the whole thing at once."

TJ scribbled. "And I'll set up an anonymous voice line for *Unfiltered*. People can call, tell a one-minute truth. We cut out names, drop clips."

Dre leaned forward. "Gametime stuff. Bathroom mirrors. Sticky notes with three words: *You're not alone*. We'll see how fast 'positive messaging' feels when positivity isn't branded."

Nyla smiled. "And kindness drops. Hygiene kits in the nurse's office with a sign: 'No questions asked.' We'll ask Ms. Calderon to help us source quietly."

"You're serious," Dre said, impressed.

"This isn't about likes," Nyla replied. "It's about dignity."

TJ flipped the page. "Launch moment?"

Nyla's eyes went to Dre's helmet. "Friday night," she said before she could talk herself out of it.

Dre's brow shot up. "Halftime? You want to get me benched and suspended in the same minute?"

"Not on the field," she said. "On the screens. The Mask Ball promo loop runs on the stadium monitors. We replace it for sixty seconds with a montage of the voices. No faces. Just truth with the words **UNMASK YOUR POWER** at the end. Then it flips back before anyone can stop it."

TJ looked like he'd just been given his birthday and a puzzle. "I can do that. The AV booth is behind the press box. I know a guy."

Dre stared at the newsprint, jaw working, then nodded once. "If we do this, it can't be a stunt. It has to land somewhere."

"It will," Nyla said. "A QR code to the story wall. The nurse's office. Counselors who actually listen."

They were quiet again, but it wasn't awkward. It felt like the last inhale before a first note.

The doorknob rattled.

All three froze. TJ snapped the newsprint pad shut, slid it beneath a stack of matte boards. Nyla closed her sketchbook so fast the elastic band slapped. Dre grabbed his helmet, the old reflex returning like muscle memory.

The door opened. Liana stood there, framed in gold light, clipboard at her side, expression unreadable.

"I figured you'd be here," she said.

No one answered.

She walked in, shut the door with a soft click, and set the clipboard on a table. Up close, the polish had fine cracks—nothing you'd see onstage, everything you'd notice under the wrong kind of light.

"I should report you," she said. "They're already looking."

"Then why didn't you bring them?" TJ asked.

Liana exhaled, something like frustration—something like relief—passing through her face. "Because I'm not sure you're wrong."

Dre's grip on the helmet loosened. "Then help us."

Her laugh was small and bitter. "You think I can just switch teams? I am the Standard."

"You're a person," Nyla said. "Pick that first."

The room listened to the clock. Liana looked at each of them in turn, eyes landing last on the newsprint pad TJ hadn't hidden quite perfectly enough. She lifted the corner and read the top line—**The Mask Society — Code**—then let it fall.

"Friday night?" she said.

TJ's eyes flickered. "What about Friday night?"

Liana ignored him. "If you're going to do something that loud, you'd better have your facts straight and your exit path clear. The press box door is alarmed after halftime. If you run your little truth ad, you'll have ninety seconds before security gets there."

"How do you know that?" Dre asked.

"Because I run events," she said. "And because I'm tired."

For the first time, the clipboard looked like it weighed more than a prop.

She reached into her bag and pulled out a slim plastic card. "This gets you past the first lock in the AV corridor," she said, placing it on the table. "It expires Saturday morning."

Nyla blinked. "You're helping us?"

"I'm protecting the school," Liana said. "From its own reflection." She paused. "And I'm asking you to be careful. Truth cuts both ways."

She turned to go, then hesitated at the door. "One more thing. If you crash our screens, the Standard will come for you. They'll come for me. Make it worth it."

She left.

Silence folded back over the room, but it didn't feel like fear anymore. It felt like gravity.

TJ slid the card toward the center of the table as if they were swearing in. "Well," he said softly. "Welcome to the Mask Society."

Dre set his helmet beside the card, a quiet offering. "Friday," he said. "We play for real."

Nyla placed her sketchbook on top, fingers resting on the red words that had started all of it.

Unmask Your Power.

Outside, a whistle blew on the practice field. Inside, three students chose the kind of game that didn't keep score.

CHAPTER FOUR

THE NIGHT OF TRUTH

Friday night at Riverstone felt electric.

Floodlights blazed over the field like stadium stars, spilling white fire over a sea of students in crimson and gold. The air smelled like popcorn, turf, and anticipation — the holy trinity of high school glory.

For most people, it was just game night.

For Nyla, it was revolution night.

She sat high in the stands, hood pulled up, phone off, sketchbook tucked under her arm. Her heart thudded in rhythm with the drumline as she scanned the crowd for TJ. He was already moving — somewhere behind the press box, laptop and access card in hand, a ghost in the system.

Across the field, Dre Vega ran warmups with mechanical precision. Every throw perfect. Every smile practiced. The mask, flawless.

But under the helmet, he was counting the minutes until halftime.

In the press box, the school's media techs ran the usual pregame show — sponsor slides, alumni shoutouts, and the *Mask Ball* promo looping every fifteen minutes. None of them noticed when one file quietly replaced another.

TJ worked fast. His fingers flew across the keyboard, pulse syncing with the crowd's roar. The program's code flashed warnings — access denied, then granted.

He whispered, "Come on, come on," as the loading bar inched forward.

Outside, Nyla checked her watch. Two minutes to halftime.

She pulled out her sketchbook, flipping to a blank page. Her hands trembled, but her lines didn't. She drew what she saw — the crowd, the masks, the light bouncing off Dre's helmet like a mirror.

Beside her, Liana Cruz appeared, still in her *Swagger Standard* jacket, clipboard clutched tight.

"You sure about this?" she asked quietly.

Nyla didn't look up. "No. That's how I know it matters."

Liana stared out at the field. "They're going to know it was us."

"Maybe that's okay," Nyla said. "Maybe it's time someone stopped pretending."

Liana's laugh was small, almost sad. "You sound like me before I learned better."

"Or like you before you stopped believing it could change," Nyla said gently.

The marching band thundered, signaling halftime. The crowd cheered.

Dre jogged off the field, chest heaving. Coach Ruiz slapped his shoulder pads.

"Good work, Vega. Keep the energy up."

"Yes, sir."

He waited until the coach turned before slipping toward the tunnel. Helmet in hand, sweat slick on his forehead, he headed straight for the press box stairs.

He found TJ crouched by the door, cords tangled around his ankle, laptop screen glowing with lines of code.

"Ready?" Dre asked.

"Almost." TJ's voice was tight. "I set it to auto-play, but if security cuts the power, we're done."

"They won't," Dre said, trying to sound like the leader he used to be.

But even he wasn't sure.

The clock hit 00:00 on the halftime scoreboard. The announcer's voice echoed:

"Ladies and gentlemen, stay in your seats for a special presentation from the *Swagger Standard*."

Then the screen flickered.

A hush fell over the stadium.

The *Mask Ball* promo vanished.

Black screen.

Then — white text.

"This is not a protest. It's a mirror."

Gasps rippled through the crowd.

One by one, voices filled the speakers — distorted, untraceable, but real:

"I'm tired of pretending I'm okay when I'm not."

"I act confident because if I don't, they'll eat me alive."

"I skipped lunch this week to afford deodorant."

"My swagger is survival."

Then Nyla's voice, steady and clear:

"We wear masks to stay safe. But what if safe isn't the same as free?"

The crowd was frozen. No movement. No cheers. Just quiet. The kind of quiet that only truth can make.

Then, images — quick flashes of student artwork, hand-drawn masks cracking open, revealing faces of every shade, expression, and story.

At the bottom of the screen, glowing red letters:

#UnmaskYourPower

Then black again.

The entire sequence had lasted less than sixty seconds.

The silence after felt longer.

Then — applause.

Not loud. Not wild. But real.

A few claps, then more. Some students stood. Some teachers didn't.

In the booth, TJ hit the kill switch just as the door banged open.

Security guards poured in, flashlights sweeping.

"Step away from the computer!"

Dre raised his hands. "It's done," he said. "You're too late."

In the stands, Liana grabbed Nyla's hand. "We need to move."

"Not yet," Nyla said, eyes on the field.

Dre walked out of the tunnel to a stadium half cheering, half whispering. He didn't wave. He didn't smile. He just walked to the fifty-yard line and took off his helmet.

The crowd gasped. No one ever took off their helmet midgame.

He lifted it high, then set it down on the turf like he was laying something heavy to rest.

Then he jogged back to his teammates, ignoring the coaches shouting his name.

After the game, the school buzzed like a beehive.

Phones blew up with clips of the screen hack — some supportive, some furious.

One teacher called it *brilliant*. Another called it *dangerous*.

The principal called an emergency meeting for Monday.

But the students… they were alive.

Something had cracked open, and the light wasn't going back in.

Nyla sat in her room past midnight, sketchbook open to a new page. She drew the stadium — small faces under big lights — and at the center, a mask dissolving into smoke.

Her mom knocked softly. "Still up, baby?"

"Yeah."

"Everything okay?"

Nyla hesitated. "I think so. I did something big."

Her mom smiled faintly. "Big things scare people at first. Doesn't mean they're wrong."

When she left, Nyla looked back at the page. She wrote across the top:

Truth always finds a screen.

Meanwhile, TJ sat at his desk, editing audio for the next *Unfiltered* drop. His inbox overflowed with anonymous messages — students sending their stories.

He uploaded the file titled **"The Night We Unmasked"** and hit publish.

And Dre?

He faced the music.

Coach Ruiz called him in before sunrise.

"You humiliated this program," Coach said. "Do you know what kind of head-lines—"

Dre interrupted, calm. "Coach, you told me to keep the huddle together. I did. I just changed who was in it."

The coach didn't answer. He just pointed to the door. "Hand in your jersey."

Dre placed it on the desk, walked out lighter than he'd felt in years.

 Liana, meanwhile, met Nyla in the art room after school that Monday.

She shut the door quietly.

"You know they're starting an investigation," she said. "They're checking camera logs."

"I know."

Liana looked at her, conflicted. "You could deny it. They don't have proof."

Nyla smiled softly. "They don't need it. They already saw it."

Liana hesitated, then nodded. "You know what's wild? They've already sold out of tickets to the Mask Ball. Everyone wants to see what happens next."

"Then maybe that's where it really starts," Nyla said. "When the masks come off for real."

That night, Nyla's phone buzzed.

A notification: *#UnmaskYourPower — Trending in Houston.*

She laughed quietly, disbelief mixing with pride.

This had started with a sketch.

Now it was a movement.

She texted TJ and Dre one word: **"We did it."**

TJ replied: **"No. We started it."**

And he was right.

Because even as the school scrambled to regain control, something deeper had already spread — a wildfire of honesty burning through the filters and false smiles.

The Mask Society wasn't just three students anymore.

It was a hundred voices, a thousand eyes, a truth too loud to erase.

CHAPTER FIVE:

THE CONSEQUENCES

Monday morning arrived like a storm.

The air at Riverstone felt different — too still, too quiet — like the school was holding its breath. Posters were gone again, but not fast enough. You could still see faint tape marks and ripped corners where the *#UnmaskYourPower* messages had been posted over the weekend.

Security guards stood at every hallway intersection.

Teachers whispered in corners.

Students avoided eye contact with anyone who might look like they "knew something."

For the first time in years, Riverstone High didn't know how to act.

Nyla felt it the moment she walked in.

Her name wasn't on the morning announcements, but the way heads turned said enough.

Some looks were curious. Others cold. A few quietly proud.

She clutched her sketchbook tight against her chest and walked faster.

Every step echoed louder than it should have.

When she reached her locker, she found a folded note tucked through the vent.

It read:

"You made me feel seen. Thank you.

– Someone who was tired of pretending."

Nyla's eyes stung. She folded it gently and slipped it into her sketchbook like a prayer.

By second period, the loudspeaker clicked on.

"Students, please be advised," said the principal's measured voice, "that Friday night's unauthorized digital display is under investigation. Anyone found involved will face disciplinary action, including possible suspension. We encourage all students to focus on learning and remember — Riverstone's strength is unity."

The line went silent.

Unity. The word hit differently now.

It sounded more like obedience.

At lunch, Nyla spotted TJ sitting alone at the back table, hood up, headphones in.

She slid into the seat beside him, keeping her voice low.

"Did you hear the announcement?"

"Yeah." He didn't look up. "They called my mom this morning. Tech department traced the file to a student laptop. Lucky for me, mine was 'borrowed.'"

"Borrowed?"

He smirked. "Liana checked it out under the *Standard* account. Guess that makes us all equal suspects."

Nyla exhaled. "She covered us."

"She bought us time," TJ said. "But not much."

Across the room, Liana entered the cafeteria — clipboard gone, hair pulled into a loose ponytail. She looked less like the polished president and more like a real person for once.

The room quieted as she passed. People didn't know whether to thank her or fear her.

She sat with them, uninvited but not unwelcome.

"You two look terrible," she said softly.

"Thanks," TJ muttered. "We're trendsetters."

Liana cracked a tired smile. "Principal Harlow's calling for a disciplinary review. He wants to make an example."

"Of who?" Nyla asked.

Liana's voice dropped. "Probably you, Dre, and me. I told him the broadcast team was testing new media software, but he doesn't buy it."

When the lunch bell rang, Nyla stepped into the hallway just as Dre appeared — still in partial uniform, helmet tucked under his arm, expression unreadable.

"Coach benched me," he said before she could ask. "Said I 'made the game political.'"

"That's ridiculous."

"Yeah. But I think I'm okay with it."

He leaned against the lockers, exhaling. "You know what's wild? People keep thanking me. The same ones who used to laugh at my 'swagger.' It's like the whole school woke up, but now they don't know what to do with the light."

Nyla studied him. He looked different — lighter somehow, even with the weight of everything hanging over them.

"Do you regret it?" she asked.

Dre shook his head. "You don't regret telling the truth. You just wish you'd told it sooner."

That afternoon, they were summoned to the principal's office.

Principal Harlow sat behind his desk, hands folded, smile tight as a rubber band.

Three chairs waited across from him. The room smelled faintly of coffee and authority.

He gestured for them to sit.

"Ms. James. Mr. Vega. Ms. Cruz. I'm sure you understand why you're here."

"Yes, sir," Liana said. Her tone was calm, professional, almost bored — her signature armor.

Harlow adjusted his glasses. "Friday's incident was a serious breach of school protocol. Tampering with district property, unauthorized broadcasting, and the spread of divisive messaging — that's not what Riverstone stands for."

"With respect," Nyla said quietly, "the messages weren't divisive. They were honest."

"Honesty without permission," Harlow said, "is still misconduct."

Dre leaned forward. "So is pretending everything's fine when it isn't."

The principal's expression hardened. "Watch your tone, Mr. Vega."

TJ wasn't there — no one knew where he was — but his words might as well have been echoing in the room: *Truth cuts both ways.*

Harlow sighed. "Here's what's going to happen. You'll each serve two weeks of disciplinary suspension — off-campus. You'll also issue a formal apology to the school community. Publicly. I'll help you prepare the statement."

"I'm not apologizing for asking people to be real," Nyla said before she could stop herself.

Liana's eyes flicked toward her — warning, respect, fear — all at once.

Harlow leaned back. "Then perhaps your future at Riverstone will need reevaluation."

The silence in the room stretched until the bell outside shattered it.

"Think carefully," Harlow said. "You have twenty-four hours."

After school, the three of them met in the art room.

No guards. No speeches. Just exhaustion.

"I'm not signing their statement," Nyla said.

"Neither am I," Dre added.

Liana sat at the desk, head in her hands. "If we all refuse, they'll expel us."

"Maybe that's what it takes," Nyla said softly. "Maybe that's how we win."

Liana lifted her head. "By losing everything?"

"By proving that truth doesn't belong to them," Nyla said. "It belongs to everyone who needs it."

That night, TJ called them on video chat. His screen was dim, voice low.

"I heard," he said. "They're trying to scare you. But something's happening outside this school. People are reposting the video — adults, other students, even teachers from other districts. The story's out."

"Out how?" Liana asked.

"Local news picked it up," TJ said. "Headline: *Students at Riverstone High Challenge Perfection Culture.'* They're calling you leaders."

Nyla blinked. "Leaders?"

"Yeah. The Dignity Initiative shared the clip on their feed this morning — said it's an example of student-led dignity work."

Liana smiled faintly. "You're telling me a nonprofit just turned us into a case study?"

"Pretty much," TJ said. "And guess what? There's a petition. Students want Riverstone to add a mental health and dignity forum next semester — with us hosting."

Dre grinned. "Guess the huddle got bigger."

The next morning, Principal Harlow's email went out schoolwide:

"In light of recent events, disciplinary actions will be paused pending district review.

We remain committed to student voice and integrity at Riverstone."

Rumor had it the superintendent had received too many emails to ignore.

When Nyla arrived at school, something new covered the walls.

Not graffiti. Not rebellion.

Hundreds of **paper masks**, all hand-cut by students.

Each one had a handwritten message:

"My mask: perfection."

"My mask: silence."

"My mask: always smiling."

"Taking it off today."

It wasn't defiance. It was reflection — and the faculty didn't stop it.

Liana met Nyla at her locker, holding a single mask that read:

"My mask: control."

She smiled, tears in her eyes. "I think we won."

Nyla shook her head gently. "No. We just reminded them how to breathe."

After school, Dre, TJ, and Nyla stood on the football field where it had all started.

No crowd this time. No screens. Just sky.

"I don't know what happens next," Dre said.

"Neither do I," Nyla admitted.

TJ grinned. "That's what makes it real."

They stood in silence for a long moment, then Nyla opened her sketchbook one last time.

She drew three figures standing under stadium lights, faces clear, shadows gone.

Beneath it, she wrote:

Truth doesn't shout. It echoes.

That night, *Unfiltered* uploaded its final episode of the semester.

TJ's voice filled the headphones of hundreds of Riverstone students:

"This isn't about rebellion. It's about reflection.

We're not fighting our school. We're helping it see us.

So take off the mask — not to break rules,

but to breathe again.

Because the only real swagger

is honesty."

The audio faded.

And in homes, bedrooms, buses, and school hallways across Houston,

students listened — quietly, bravely, unmasked.

CHAPTER SIX

THE MASK BALL

Winter came late to Houston that year — a soft chill that made the gym lights feel warmer, more golden than usual. The banner hanging above the stage read:

RIVERSTONE MASK BALL: CELEBRATING CONFIDENCE & COMMUNITY.

But this year, nobody was really here for confidence.

They were here for truth.

Rows of paper lanterns swayed from the ceiling. The DJ played mellow beats instead of pop hits, and the school's art club had covered the walls with hundreds of student-made masks — each one cracked open down the middle, painted with words like *Resilience, Courage, Healing,* and *Dignity.*

The old Riverstone would've turned the night into a fashion contest.

This one felt more like a story being finished — and rewritten at the same time.

Nyla stood by the punch table, dress simple but elegant — a deep red that matched the ribbon still tied to her backpack zipper. She traced the fabric, thinking of her mom's words from that first day: *You don't need new to look new. You just need purpose.*

Tonight, purpose shimmered in the air.

"Still weird seeing all this?" TJ asked, appearing beside her, adjusting his tie like he didn't quite know how to exist in formal clothes.

Nyla smiled. "We started this in a stairwell."

"Now we're center stage," he said, nodding toward the podium where Liana was talking with teachers and administrators. "Principal Harlow even asked us to speak."

"That part still feels weird."

TJ grinned. "Truth usually does."

Across the gym, Dre Vega walked in, wearing his letterman jacket for the first time since the suspension. The crowd parted for him — not out of fear, but out of quiet respect. Even Coach Ruiz nodded when their eyes met.

"Quarterback returns," TJ whispered.

"Quarterback evolved," Nyla said.

Dre approached, hands in pockets. "They're letting us speak after the dance competition. Guess honesty isn't the warm-up act anymore."

"You ready?" Nyla asked.

"Born ready," Dre said. "Just didn't know it until now."

When the lights dimmed, the chatter hushed. Principal Harlow stepped to the mic, his tone formal but softer than usual.

"Tonight isn't about who's wearing what," he said. "It's about who we've become. Riverstone High is proud of its students — especially those who remind us that confidence is not about image, but integrity."

The crowd clapped politely. Then he looked toward the side of the stage.

"And now, I'd like to welcome three students who helped us start an important conversation."

The applause grew — real this time.

Nyla, Dre, and TJ walked onto the stage together. The microphone squeaked once, as if nervous too.

Nyla went first. Her voice trembled at first but steadied quickly.

"When I came here, I thought swagger meant pretending — being louder than my fears, hiding what hurt. I drew a mask because I didn't know how else to say I was tired. But then other people saw themselves in it. And suddenly, we weren't alone."

She paused, scanning the faces in the crowd — students, teachers, even her mom near the back.

"I'm not here to tell anyone to break rules," she said. "I'm just here to remind us that sometimes following the right truth matters more than following the easy path. The Mask Society isn't about rebellion. It's about realness."

Applause rose like a wave — quiet, powerful, lasting.

Dre took the mic next.

"I used to think swagger meant never showing weakness," he said. "But I've learned strength isn't about how long you can fake it. It's how fast you can admit you're human."

He looked out at the football players in the crowd. "We've all worn masks — fear, anger, pride. But you can't lead people if you're hiding from them."

He nodded toward Nyla and TJ. "These two showed me that truth can be a team sport."

The gym erupted.

Even Coach Ruiz stood, clapping.

Finally, TJ stepped forward. His voice had that same radio calm — confident but real.

"I'm the guy who records everything," he said. "But for a long time, I was scared of my own voice. So I hid behind the mic. Then I realized — truth doesn't need a filter, it needs a home. And now, *Unfiltered* isn't just a podcast. It's what this school became when we stopped pretending."

He lifted a small remote and clicked a slide onto the projector screen behind them.

A collage appeared — dozens of student-submitted drawings, notes, and photos of cracked masks.

Across the top: **'Our Faces, Our Truth.'**

Underneath, one phrase:

Unmask Your Power.

The crowd rose. Not all at once, not perfectly timed — just naturally.

Applause thundered, phones lifted to record, tears glistened.

Liana walked onstage, clipboard-free for once. "For the record," she said into the mic, "this is the best 'Standard' we've ever had."

The gym roared with laughter and cheers.

Later, the DJ shifted into slow music. Students danced — some awkwardly, some fearlessly, some in groups laughing through tears.

Nyla stood near the stage steps, watching. Dre approached, holding two cups of punch.

"You realize this might be the first school dance where nobody's competing?" he said.

"Maybe that's the real revolution," Nyla replied.

"Or maybe it's the start of normal."

"Normal's overrated," she said. "Honest feels better."

They clinked cups like victory bells.

Toward the end of the night, Principal Harlow found Nyla by the art wall.

He looked older somehow, humbled.

"I owe you an apology," he said quietly. "I was protecting the school's reputation, but you were protecting its soul."

Nyla smiled gently. "Thank you, sir. I think we're both still learning."

He nodded. "Keep making us uncomfortable, Ms. James. That's how we grow."

When the music ended, students began removing their decorative masks one by one, placing them on the table near the exit.

By the time the lights came up, hundreds of masks covered the table — a mosaic of what the year had been.

TJ, Dre, and Nyla stood together, looking at them.

"It's wild," TJ said. "All those faces, all those stories."

Dre nodded. "All those hearts that decided to stop hiding."

Nyla ran her fingers across one mask — painted half-blue, half-gold, a faint crack down the middle.

"I used to think I drew that crack to show what was broken," she said. "But now I think it was showing where the light gets in."

Outside, under the cool December air, they walked toward the parking lot. The stadium lights were still glowing faintly from the earlier game.

"Feels like an ending," Dre said.

"Maybe," Nyla replied. "But not *the* ending."

TJ grinned. "Every movement needs a sequel."

Nyla laughed. "We'll call it growth, not a sequel."

They stopped at the school's mural — the one painted weeks ago by the art club after the investigation ended.

It showed three silhouettes under the words:

THE MASK SOCIETY: SWAGGER REDEFINED.

Below it, smaller words in red paint:

Truth doesn't divide — it connects.

They stood in silence, letting the moment breathe.

Cars honked in the distance. The world went on, but something inside each of them had settled — not finished, just ready.

Back home, Nyla opened her sketchbook one last time.

She drew the scene as she remembered it: hundreds of masks on the table, students laughing, teachers smiling.

At the bottom of the page, she wrote:

"We started with cracks.

We ended with light."

She closed the book, exhaled, and whispered —

"Swagger isn't what they said it was.

It's what we became."

CHAPTER SEVEN:

THE RIPPLE BEGINS

Spring sunlight cut across Riverstone's courtyard, bouncing off lockers and fresh paint.

For the first time since the halftime night, the school didn't feel tense — it felt awake.

The old "Swagger Standard" posters had come down for good. In their place, the art club had painted a long, winding mural — hundreds of student-made masks swirling into one colorful wave. At its center, the words:

UNMASK YOUR POWER.

"Looks like it's real now," TJ said, filming on his phone for *Unfiltered 2.0.*

He zoomed in on students adding their own paper masks to the wall.

"This was supposed to be a secret society," Dre joked, tossing a basketball between his hands. "Now even the freshmen know the code."

Nyla smiled but felt the weight of his words. *Secret* had turned public, and public had a way of getting complicated.

Liana appeared with a clipboard — yes, still a clipboard — but this time it carried flyers for **The Dignity Initiative.**

"They want us to run the first student partnership pilot," she said, eyes bright. "Art show, hygiene-kit fundraiser, and school-wide story wall. Houston Gazette already asking for a quote."

"A quote?" Nyla repeated. "Since when are we news?"

"Since people decided we are," Liana said.

That week became a blur.

Local reporters visited art class; teachers smiled through interviews; students who'd once mocked them now volunteered to paint, post, record.

The cafeteria bulletin board overflowed with messages:

"My mask: pretending to be fine."

"My mask: acting confident."

"Taking it off today."

It felt right. It also felt… *loud.*

At night, Nyla scrolled through social media under her blanket, reading comments.

Most were supportive.

Some weren't.

"Why are schools letting kids talk about emotions on campus?"

"Focus on grades, not feelings."

"This is another woke fad."

She locked her phone and stared at the ceiling.

Truth had gone viral — but so had misunderstanding.

Friday, The Dignity Initiative representatives arrived — a small team in black shirts with the white dove logo. They brought boxes of hygiene kits and stacks of books from

The Dignity Collection.

The gym buzzed with energy as students packed supplies while writing short affirmations on cards:

"You are seen."

"You matter."

"Keep your head high."

When the director of Dignity Initiative, spoke, her voice filled the bleachers with warmth.

"What these students did," she said, glancing toward Nyla's group, "wasn't rebellion — it was leadership. Dignity begins when truth finds courage."

Applause rolled through the room.

For the first time, Nyla saw adults listening — really listening — and that felt like victory.

But by Monday, victory came with shadows.

A district email circulated: *All outside partnerships must be reviewed for content alignment.*

Rumor said a few parents had complained about "controversial messaging."

Liana frowned reading it. "Content alignment? That's code for control."

Dre shrugged. "We knew the spotlight wouldn't stay friendly."

TJ uploaded a quiet episode of *Unfiltered* that night titled **"When the Mic Gets Heavy."**

His closing words stuck with Nyla:

"The moment you're heard, someone decides you're too loud."

Two days later, a TV van pulled up outside the school.

A reporter wanted to film a segment called *Teen Truth-Tellers or Troublemakers?*

Coach Ruiz told Dre to keep his distance.

Principal Harlow avoided cameras entirely.

Only Nyla spoke — short, careful sentences about honesty, art, and dignity.

But when the clip aired that evening, her words were sliced between commentary.

The headline read: **"Student Group Pushes Feelings Over Academics."**

Her mom muted the TV. "You told your truth," she said gently. "They just didn't listen right."

Still, Nyla felt exposed, like her sketchbook had been opened to a page she hadn't finished.

By the end of April, the movement had momentum — and enemies she couldn't see.

Teachers loved it.

Students swore by it.

But emails buzzed between district offices, and whispers started about "policy reviews."

One afternoon, as the group met in the art room, a custodian paused by the door.

"Y'all did something big," he said. "Just remember — every ripple hits a shore."

Then he walked away, leaving silence behind.

Nyla looked at the mural through the window — bright, bold, unstoppable — and felt the first pull of a tide she hadn't planned for.

That night, she drew a single image: a wave hitting a wall, splitting into dozens of smaller waves.

At the bottom she wrote:

"The ripple has begun.

Let's see who tries to stop it."

CHAPTER EIGHT

THE SPOTLIGHT BURNS

By mid-April, Riverstone's hallways looked like a commercial for authenticity — posters, podcasts, and news cameras capturing kids "being real."

But the air had changed.

What started as a whisper of freedom now hummed with expectation.

Everyone wanted a piece of The Mask Society.

Not everyone wanted the truth.

"Smile for Channel 7!" the reporter called.

Nyla forced one. The camera light stung her eyes as she stood in front of the mural that used to feel like hers. Behind her, a crowd of students posed with crafted masks, glitter catching sunlight.

The reporter grinned. "So, Nyla, would you say your message is about feelings over academics?"

Her stomach twisted. "It's about dignity," she said carefully. "When students feel seen, they do better in everything — including academics."

The reporter nodded like he'd caught something juicy. "But you *do* think schools should change what they teach, right?"

"I think they should remember *who* they teach."

The cameraman lowered the lens. "Perfect," he said. Nyla felt cold.

Later that night, the clip aired with the caption:

"Teen Group Challenges School Priorities."

It wasn't a lie, exactly. It was just smaller than the truth.

Dre watched it from the locker room. His teammates stared at him over their phones.

"Bro, they turned you into a protest," Marcus said.

Dre didn't answer. He'd already gotten the email from a recruiter:

We value your leadership, but we need players focused on performance, not publicity.

He crumpled the message and tossed his phone into his locker.

Performance had always been his mask. Now he wasn't sure what face to wear instead.

At school, TJ tried to keep control through *Unfiltered.*

He launched a three-part series called **"Behind the Masks,"** interviewing teachers and students about honesty and burnout.

But the more he recorded, the more pressure he felt to sound perfect — polished truth instead of raw truth.

When one of his guests, a quiet sophomore named Renee, froze mid-interview and said she wasn't ready to talk, TJ turned off the recorder without a word.

Later, when the producer from a local station asked him to "use her breakdown for impact," he said no.

That night, he deleted every draft and sat in the dark, questioning who he'd become.

Meanwhile, Liana was drowning in logistics.

She'd turned the *Day of Dignity* idea into a district-wide event — hygiene-kit drives, speaker panels, art showcases.

It should've been triumph.

Instead, it felt like crisis management.

Her inbox filled with emails from principals asking for permission slips and "content guidelines."

She spent hours rewriting flyers to sound less "emotional."

When Nyla walked into the library one afternoon, she found Liana surrounded by crumpled drafts.

"They want me to replace 'Unmask Your Power' with 'Find Your Strength,'" Liana said bitterly. "It's cleaner, they said. Less political."

"Are we political now?" Nyla asked.

Liana sighed. "Anything honest is political to someone."

The next morning, Dre didn't show up to class.

Rumor spread that he'd quit the team for good.

Nyla found him sitting on the bleachers after school, still in his practice gear, staring at the empty field.

"They said I lost focus," he said quietly. "Maybe I did. I started seeing more than the scoreboard."

He looked at her. "Tell me it was worth it."

Nyla sat beside him. "If it wasn't, we'd still be pretending."

They watched the sun slide behind the goalposts. The silence between them wasn't heavy — just honest.

By the end of the week, things started to crack.

Social media turned the movement into trends.

Hashtags like *#UnmaskChallenge* flooded feeds — kids recording "before and after" shots of taking off fake smiles, then adding filters to make it look artistic.

It was everything The Mask Society *wasn't*.

"People love the message when it looks good," TJ said, scrolling angrily. "They don't want the messy part."

Liana slammed her laptop shut. "Maybe we should pause. Regroup. It's spinning out."

"No," Nyla said. "If we back off, they'll rewrite us again. We just have to remind them what it means."

"Then say it," Dre said. "Say it loud enough that no one else can own it."

Nyla looked around the art room — their unofficial headquarters — and took a slow breath.

Maybe it was time to speak, not just draw.

Two days later, they hosted a live assembly — the first *Mask Society Forum.*

Teachers sat in folding chairs. Students packed the gym.

No microphones, no scripts. Just a circle of chairs in the center.

Nyla stood first. "We started this to stop pretending," she said. "But somewhere along the way, we got packaged, too. So here's us — no edits."

Dre spoke next, voice low. "We messed up, sometimes. We talked big and forgot to listen. We said 'be real' and still hid behind what people wanted us to be. But we're learning."

Liana nodded, adding, "You can't trademark truth. So stop expecting us to be perfect."

The gym stayed quiet for a heartbeat, then applause rose — messy, uneven, human.

In that moment, Nyla remembered why they'd started: not to trend, not to teach, but to feel whole.

That night, they sat outside the school beneath the mural's glow, exhausted but lighter.

TJ held up his recorder. "Final thought of the day?"

Nyla smiled. "Being seen isn't the goal. Being understood is."

He clicked *stop.*

Across town, though, another conversation was beginning — in emails, on radio shows, and in parent-teacher meetings titled *"The Line Between Guidance and Indoctrination."*

Riverstone didn't know it yet, but the spotlight that burned brightest was about to turn into fire.

CHAPTER NINE:

THE DIVIDE

By May, the movement had a name in the city.

Some people called it **The Ripple**. Others called it **a problem**.

The morning it broke, Nyla was pouring cereal when the TV over the kitchen counter flashed a panel of well-dressed adults debating teens they'd never met.

"…and this so-called 'Mask Society' is teaching kids to distrust authority," a commentator said, smiling like concern was a brand. "Since when is school a therapy session?"

Another guest shook her head. "It's not therapy. It's activism disguised as classroom culture. Parents deserve a say."

Nyla muted the volume, heart thudding. Her mom, grading papers at the table, didn't look up.

"You okay?" she asked softly.

"I don't know," Nyla said. She wasn't used to being talked about by people who refused to say her name.

Her phone buzzed: a screenshot from TJ — a petition with a red header.

Protect Our Schools: Remove Mask Society Content from Campuses.

Below it, bullet points: *undermines discipline, promotes negative self-focus, politicizes mental health*. Ten thousand signatures and climbing.

Another text arrived, from Liana: **School board added a "public comment" session. Tonight. We should speak.**

Then one from Dre: **They're coming for us. We show up.**

Nyla swallowed and typed: **We tell the truth.**

At lunch, Riverstone felt split down an invisible seam. One hallway had flyers for **Day of Dignity** and a hygiene drive; the other posted a PTA notice: **"Return to Academics — Keep Politics Out."**

Dre leaned against the trophy case, reading both like they were plays to memorize.

"You see the radio hit?" he asked as Nyla approached. "They called me 'the activist quarterback.'"

"You earned it," she said.

"I didn't ask for it." He glanced toward the field outside. "Scholarship rep emailed my coach. Wants to know if I'm going to be a 'distraction' on their campus."

Nyla felt the floor tilt. "Dre…"

He shrugged, that careful kind that kept feelings from spilling. "There are worse reasons to get benched than telling the truth."

Liana joined them, eyes shadowed from too little sleep. She held up a printed agenda, the district's crest stamped at the top.

"Item 4C," she said. "Public comment on 'student-initiated messaging.' It's us without saying us."

"What's the rule?" TJ asked, appearing with his recorder already in his hand.

"Two minutes per speaker," Liana said. "Thirty seconds to finish when the red light blinks."

He tapped the mic. "Plenty of time to tell a whole life."

By evening, the boardroom hallways were thick with bodies and opinions. Suits and blazers clustered near the door; The Dignity Initiative T-shirts and team hoodies stood in small, determined groups. Handmade signs peeked above heads:

SEE STUDENTS, NOT SCORES

DIGNITY ≠ DEFIANCE

KEEP SCHOOL SAFE FROM POLITICS

Principal Harlow stood near the aisle, tie tight, expression careful. When he saw the four of them, his mouth softened.

"Be calm," he murmured. "Be specific. Facts win the room."

"Facts don't always win the edit," TJ said, raising his recorder.

A woman in pearls brushed past them, perfume sharp. "Children should be learning calculus, not confessing feelings in the hallway," she said to no one in particular, and to everyone at once.

A dad in a ball cap answered from three feet away. "My son started eating lunch again because of those kids."

The gavel fell. The board took their seats. A camera light from a local station clicked on.

"Public comment is now open," the chair said. "Please remember: we discuss ideas, not individuals."

The first speaker strode to the mic with a binder and certainty.

"I'm here on behalf of the **Parents for Order** coalition," she announced. "While we support kindness, we oppose the Mask Society content that shames students who choose excellence and discipline. My daughter shouldn't have to walk past walls that tell her she's fake because she's confident."

Applause crackled from one side of the room. Nyla felt the air tighten.

A teacher stepped up next. "I've taught here eighteen years," he said. "I've never seen students show each other this much care. Grades went up in my class because kids stopped pretending and started asking for help."

Polite claps. A few eyerolls.

A man in a crisp blazer approached the mic, jaw set. "This is a public school, not a social experiment. If my son struggles, that's our family conversation — not hallway graffiti."

"Then why didn't you have it?" someone muttered behind Nyla. She didn't turn.

The chair called, "Please, order."

Name after name, the room swayed: for them, against them, for some idea of them that didn't match their faces. Nyla watched the red light blink speakers off mid-sentence, felt time become a thing with teeth.

Then the chair said, "Students, you'll have your turn now."

TJ went first. He didn't stand at the podium right away. He set his recorder on the edge of it like a talisman, looked at the board, then at the crowd.

"I'm the voice behind *Unfiltered*," he said. "I hid because I was scared. Not of truth — of being laughed at for needing it. Since we started, I've received 412 messages from students across this district. None of them say 'tear school down.' They say, 'Please see me.'"

He pressed a button. A single, anonymized sentence filled the speakers, warped just enough to protect the kid who'd said it:

"I've stopped bringing deodorant because we can't afford it and I eat lunch in the bathroom."

Gasps. A chair scraped. Someone whispered, "That's my school."

TJ clicked the recorder off. "That's what you're voting on," he said. "Not a brand. A mirror."

Liana walked next. She didn't bring a clipboard. Her hands were empty in a way Nyla had never seen.

"I built the 'Swagger Standard,'" she said. "I thought if we taught confidence like a formula, we'd make students brave. We made them performers. The Mask Society didn't replace academics — it repaired trust. If we're afraid of what students say when we finally listen, maybe the problem isn't the students."

The applause came from both sides this time, cautious but real.

Dre took the podium. He set a folded paper on it but never looked down.

"I'm the quarterback who got benched," he began, half-smiling. "You can call it a consequence. I call it a clearance. I've never thought clearer than when I stopped trying to look invincible."

He turned slightly, addressing the parents row. "I get it. You want school to be safe. So do we. Safe isn't quiet. Safe is a place you can tell the truth and not be punished for it. That's all we did. That's all we ask."

Nyla's chest felt too small for her heart. She stepped up last. The microphone wobbled under her fingers; she steadied it with both hands.

"My name is Nyla James," she said. "I drew the first mask because I didn't have the words."

She held up her sketchbook. The battered cover looked out of place under the chamber lights.

"I didn't come here to fight you," she said to the room. "I came to invite you. If you want your kids to focus, see them. If you want them to excel, let them be human. We're not asking you to change the math. We're asking you to change the mirror."

The red light blinked. She stopped. The room stayed very still.

Then the board chair cleared his throat. "Thank you, students." He shuffled his papers. "We appreciate the passion on both sides. The policy proposal before us is to restrict unapproved student messaging and third-party materials related to the 'Mask Society' on campus."

A murmur rolled through the crowd.

"Before we vote," the chair added, "we'll take three more comments."

A woman stood — the pearl necklace, the perfume. She walked to the mic, hands trembling just enough to betray the steel in her voice.

"My daughter cried last week because she felt like she was doing high school wrong — not good enough at being vulnerable," she said. "Don't tell us how to feel."

Nyla's stomach dropped. It was the argument she feared most: the idea that vulnerability could be another performance.

Before the chair could close comment, a thin man the color of an old baseball glove stepped forward in a custodian's polo. Nyla recognized him from the hallways, the slow tide who peeled down posters and hummed hymns under his breath.

"I clean your floors," he said, voice soft. "Been doing it fifteen years. I see the gum and the glitter and the tears. When those kids started putting notes on the walls, I thought, 'Here we go, more tape to scrape.' But then I read one. And another. And another. I saw your children telling the truth to nobody and everybody at once. I took a picture of one that said, **You are enough**, and I keep it in my wallet. On nights I work late, it reminds me why I'm here. Let the kids be kind to each other. It helps the rest of us work."

Silence. Then someone clapped. Then more. The sound gathered like rain.

The chair tapped the gavel. "We'll vote."

Hands raised. Names called. **Ayes** and **nays** dropped into the room like coins into a well.

Motion one — to ban all Mask Society materials — failed by one vote.

Motion two — to form a student-faculty working group on dignity and wellness — passed, barely.

Half the room exhaled. The other half muttered. The gavel fell again. "Meeting adjourned."

The crowd dissolved into knots of relief and frustration. A local reporter tried to corner Dre; he smiled politely and slipped past. Liana hugged the custodian with the careful gratitude of someone receiving back a piece of faith. TJ packed the recorder like it was fragile history.

Nyla stood in the aisle, dizzy with the way victory could feel like a bruise.

A woman in a denim jacket touched her arm. "My son hasn't spoken at dinner in months," she said, eyes shining. "Tonight he whispered, 'Maybe I could.' Thank you."

Nyla nodded, throat tight. "Tell him he already did."

Outside, the night smelled like cut grass and distant rain. Protest signs leaned against trash cans like tired soldiers. The four of them stood under a streetlight, faces pale gold.

"We didn't win everything," Liana said.

"We didn't come for everything," TJ answered. "We came for a door."

"It cracked," Dre said. He looked at his phone — a new email from his scholarship program with a subject line he couldn't yet bring himself to open. He locked the screen and smiled anyway. "Cracks let in light."

Nyla opened her sketchbook on the hood of a car and drew the boardroom in two strokes: a wall of faces, a small mic, a red light blinking out. Then she drew a door with light around the hinges.

Beneath it she wrote: **They called it controversy. We called it a conversation.**

Thunder mumbled far away. The four of them stood there a little longer, letting the sky practice rain, letting the city decide whether to listen.

When the first drops fell, they didn't run. They tilted their faces up and let the weather have its say.

CHAPTER TEN:

THE AFTERSHOCK

The morning after the board meeting, Riverstone felt like a storm had passed without choosing sides.

Half the students treated the vote as freedom.

The other half acted like it was failure.

Posters still clung to the hallway walls — half cheering, half accusing.

One read **"MASK SOCIETY = CHAOS,"** before someone crossed out *chaos* and scrawled *Courage* underneath.

It wasn't peace. It was aftermath.

Nyla sat in the cafeteria, her tray untouched, her phone lighting up every few seconds.

Notifications blurred into noise — comments, headlines, and arguments she didn't ask for.

"This group is brave."

"These kids are out of control."

"Keep politics out of schools."

Her name trended for the first time — not as a person, but as an argument.

TJ slid into the seat across from her, dark circles under his eyes.

"They published our emails," he said flatly.

"Who did?"

"Some blog. Everything — project notes, meeting plans, even the Dignity Drive schedule."

Nyla's stomach turned. "That's private."

"Not anymore. They're saying **The Dignity Initiative** is paying us to 'push emotional agendas.'"

"Seriously?" she said. "We're high schoolers, not lobbyists."

"Yeah, well, welcome to the news cycle."

He dropped his phone face-down and muttered, "They just made us the villains in our own story."

Across campus, Dre sat in the locker room, staring at the space where his nameplate used to hang.

Coach Ruiz leaned against the doorway. "College recruiter called again," he said quietly.

Dre looked up, expecting it.

"They're not canceling your offer. They just want 'distance' until things cool off."

Dre gave a short, bitter laugh. "So, truth is bad for the brand now?"

"Son," the coach said gently, "truth makes people uncomfortable before it sets them free."

Dre didn't answer. He just nodded, grabbed his duffel, and walked out before the silence swallowed him.

That night, the four of them met in the art room — their refuge, their headquarters.

The long table was covered with sketches, flyers, and mask fragments from old projects.

The air buzzed with unspoken fear.

Liana was the first to speak.

"They're investigating us," she said. "Emails, grants, even our mentors at **The Dignity Initiative**. Apparently, someone thinks we're being used to push an agenda."

TJ looked up sharply. "We *are* being used. By the same people twisting our story for clicks."

Nyla frowned. "They're trying to scare us."

"Maybe it's working," Liana said softly. "I haven't slept in three nights."

For a moment, no one spoke. The only sound was the hum of the art room's old fluorescent lights.

Then Dre said, "We can't let them own the narrative. We started this — we should be the ones to tell it."

TJ nodded. "We go public. Our words. Our faces. No middlemen."

Liana hesitated. "That's risky."

"So is silence," Nyla said.

She looked around the room — at the mural on the wall, the sketches, the notes that had started a movement. "If they're going to talk about us, they should at least see who we are."

Two nights later, they turned the gym into a studio.

A borrowed camera. Two ring lights. A stack of dignity kits and student art displays behind them — proof, not propaganda.

TJ adjusted the mic and said quietly, "Ready?"

Nyla nodded.

She faced the camera and spoke:

"You've heard a hundred versions of our story. Here's ours.

We're not rebels. We're students who saw our friends hiding behind silence.

We created The Mask Society to remind people that dignity isn't earned — it's human."

She gestured to the table behind her.

"These kits don't promote politics. They promote care.

They say, 'You deserve to show up tomorrow without shame.'

If that's controversial, maybe the problem isn't the students."

Dre took the mic next.

"I lost a scholarship for speaking up," he said. "And I'd still do it again.

Because pretending everything's fine doesn't make it so.

The truth doesn't ruin schools — it saves them."

Liana followed.

"We're not perfect. We argued. We got scared. But we didn't give up.

We built something that helped people breathe again.

If breathing is political, then we'll keep doing it."

TJ closed the broadcast.

"This isn't about likes or trends. It's about what happens when students stop being silent.

The Mask Society isn't rebellion. It's reflection.

And you can't cancel what's already human."

He hit *stop.*

The video went live at midnight.

By morning, it had over fifty thousand views.

By lunch, a hundred thousand.

By dinner, a statement from **The Dignity Initiative** appeared on social media:

"We stand with these students.

Dignity is not defiance.

The Mask Society represents what education can be — truth in action."

The tide began to shift. Slowly, but undeniably.

Within days, other students started posting videos with the hashtag **#IAmMask-Society** — reading poems, showing their artwork, telling small truths about anxiety, shame, or confidence.

Even teachers joined in, writing quiet notes on their classroom doors:

"This is a safe space for truth."

For the first time in weeks, Nyla felt something she hadn't felt since the chaos began

— possibility.

But the pressure hadn't vanished.

Liana was burned out, juggling calls from reporters and parents.

TJ was exhausted from defending them online.

Dre had one foot out the door, terrified his scholarship might vanish completely.

And Nyla… she couldn't draw.

Every time she opened her sketchbook, the lines came out shaky.

Truth felt heavier now that the world was watching.

That night, she wrote instead. Just one line in the corner of a page:

"Aftershocks don't destroy what's true — they reveal who stays standing."

She closed the book and exhaled.

A week later, a district email arrived:

"All student suspensions related to the Mask Society have been lifted.

Collaboration with The Dignity Initiative reinstated pending review."

It wasn't an apology, but it was enough.

When she read it aloud in the art room, Dre grinned for the first time in weeks.

TJ whooped and threw his phone in the air.

Liana covered her face, laughing through tears.

"We made it," TJ said. "Kind of."

Nyla smiled softly. "No. We *earned* it."

That evening, she returned to her sketchbook and drew four hands gripping a cracked mask — not breaking it, but holding it together.

Underneath, she wrote:

"Aftershock doesn't end the story. It makes sure it's worth telling."

For the first time in months, she felt steady — bruised, maybe, but whole.

And she knew the ripple they'd started wasn't ending here.

It was only just beginning again.

CHAPTER ELEVEN

THE STAND TOGETHER

June sunlight poured through the art-room windows like forgiveness.

For the first time in months, Riverstone felt steady again.

The district had reinstated their partnership with **The Dignity Initiative**, but the air still hummed with what the fight had cost.

Students laughed more softly now; teachers measured every word.

Healing had begun, but it limped.

Nyla refused to wait for permission.

"The board gave us our voice back," she told the group. "So let's use it."

Three weeks later, the flyers appeared:

THE DAY OF DIGNITY

Student Voices • Real Change • Presented by Riverstone High and The Dignity Initiative.

It wasn't a rally.

It was a restart.

The gym pulsed with color and noise.

Tables brimmed with hygiene kits, student art, and signup sheets for service projects.

Across the walls:

"Truth isn't trouble."

"Dignity belongs to everyone."

"No masks. No shame."

Liana paced the floor checking details, clipboardless for once.

Dre loaded boxes beside teammates who used to mock him.

TJ hovered near the mic stand, trying not to over-rehearse.

Nyla just watched — amazed that chaos could turn into choreography.

Principal Harlow opened the program.

"I thought leadership meant control," he admitted. "These students showed me it means listening."

The applause felt like sunlight after rain.

Then came the students.

Dre spoke first, jacket unzipped, nerves steady.

"I used to think swagger was armor," he said. "Turns out strength is letting people see the dents."

Liana followed. "I built rules to keep us safe. But honesty is safer than perfection."

TJ played short clips from *Unfiltered Live*: students confessing fear, friendship, forgiveness.

When the last voice faded, he said, "We're not trending. We're transforming."

Finally, Nyla took the stage.

She opened her sketchbook — the same one that started everything — revealing a drawing of four hands holding a cracked mask.

"We didn't start a protest," she said. "We started a promise — to stop pretending and start caring. If that's rebellion, then maybe the world needs more rebels."

The crowd rose, applause thundering.

Even the janitor in the back wiped his eyes.

Afterward, when the gym emptied, a woman in a silver-and-gold Dignity Initiative shirt approached them. Glitter still clung to her sleeves.

"You turned conflict into community," she said. "That's leadership."

She handed Nyla a sealed envelope.

"The Dignity Initiative is creating a Youth Leadership Fellowship — art, storytelling, outreach. We'd like the four of you to be the first class."

TJ gaped. "For real?"

"Completely," she said. "The ripple's ready for its next wave."

That night, the four sat on the front steps beneath a pink-orange sky.

The mural behind them glowed under lamplight — masks becoming open hands.

"Think people will remember this?" TJ asked.

"Someone will," Liana said.

Dre smiled. "Then we did our job."

Nyla closed her sketchbook. "Not a job," she whispered. "A beginning."

CHAPTER TWELVE:

THE LEGACY

Two years later, Riverstone High had changed forever.

The mural still spread across the main hallway, colors softened by time but bright as truth.

Beneath it, a bronze plaque read:

Dedicated to The Mask Society —

For proving that courage is contagious.

Graduation banners rippled outside.

Nyla stood under the mural, tracing one of the painted cracks.

It no longer looked broken — it looked alive.

Dre appeared beside her, taller now, confidence quiet instead of loud.

"Still drawing?" he teased.

"Still healing," she said.

Liana arrived, clipboard stamped **The Dignity Initiative Youth Council**.

"Don't laugh," she warned. "It's scheduling next week's dignity drive."

TJ followed, camera swinging. "And I'm filming it — *Unmasked: How One School Changed Everything.* The Initiative's backing it."

Nyla grinned. "Guess we really did start something."

During the ceremony, Principal Harlow's closing words brought the crowd to its feet.

"These graduates taught us that education isn't about hiding flaws — it's about honoring truth. May every school remember what they reminded us: dignity is strength."

Dre caught Nyla's eye. They both smiled.

They had survived the storm and built something the wind couldn't take.

Afterward, they gathered in the courtyard.

Liana announced she'd accepted a full-time role with The Dignity Initiative, coordinating youth storytelling programs.

TJ was off to UT Austin to expand *Unfiltered.*

Nyla planned to study art therapy.

Dre had a coaching scholarship — teaching young athletes what confidence really means.

A group of middle-schoolers approached shyly, wearing shirts that read **MASK SOCIETY — CHAPTER TWO.**

"You're the originals, right?" one asked. "We started a branch at Oakview."

They handed Nyla a folded paper:

"Because of you, our school listens."

Nyla blinked away tears. "Keep it going," she said. "It's yours now."

Later, the four posed beneath the mural one last time.

"Say it," Dre said.

Together they whispered, **"Unmask your power."**

The camera flashed, freezing the moment like proof.

That night, Nyla sat on her porch, sketchbook open to the last blank page.

She drew one final image — a cracked mask glowing from within.

Below it, she wrote:

"Legacy isn't what we leave behind.

It's what we light in others."

She thought of something the director of **The Dignity Initiative** once told them:

"Movements only matter if they outgrow the people who start them."

Nyla smiled. The movement already had.

The next morning they met for coffee before scattering to their new lives.

TJ raised his cup. "To cracks."

Liana: "To courage."

Dre: "To truth that keeps standing."

Nyla: "To every student still afraid to be seen — you already are."

They clinked cups, laughter mixing with quiet pride.

The sun rose, spilling gold across the table, and for a moment it felt like the world itself had taken off its mask.

That evening, a janitor found a handwritten note taped under the mural:

"We started with masks.

We ended with mirrors."

He smiled, folded it carefully, and kept it in his pocket — proof that even the smallest truths can echo forever.

WHEN THE MASKS CAME OFF

It started as a story.

A hallway, a drawing, a cracked mask — and a girl trying to find her voice in a place that rewarded silence.

But somewhere between the pages, it became more than fiction.

It became *a mirror*.

Every school has its version of Riverstone High.

Every student has a version of Nyla — that moment when pretending gets too heavy, when the smile stops fitting, and when truth knocks softly and asks to be let out.

When *The Mask Society* began, it wasn't rebellion. It was recognition — a reminder that real strength doesn't come from perfection; it comes from showing up as yourself, scars and all.

The truth is, some stories don't stay on paper.

They find you later — in a student afraid to raise her hand because she hasn't brushed her hair in days, or a boy too embarrassed to ask for deodorant before gym, or a classmate who hides pain behind jokes until someone finally listens.

That's why **Spirit, Inc.** exists — not as a charity, but as a promise:

That every student deserves dignity.

That no one's worth depends on their reflection.

That a hygiene kit, a story, or a single honest conversation can change the way a child sees themselves.

Because dignity isn't a luxury — it's a right.

And truth, even when it costs you, is still the most powerful kind of freedom.

If you're holding this book, you're holding part of that mission.

Every page, every purchase, every act of compassion helps us keep the ripple alive — in classrooms, locker rooms, and lunch tables where silence once ruled.

So keep drawing your cracks.

Keep speaking your truth.

Keep unmasking your power.

Because when one student finds the courage to be real,

the whole world takes a breath — and starts to heal.

— Joyce Lee

For every student who ever thought they had to hide to be accepted.

RESOURCES & WAYS TO KEEP THE RIPPLE GOING

The story of *The Mask Society* was born from real experiences of students learning to balance truth, dignity, and courage. If you connected with this story, here are ways to continue that journey — in your community and beyond.

◊ 1. Dignity & Wellness for Students

The Dignity Initiative — The Dignity Initiative is a fictional program inspired by the same goals driving real nonprofits like **Spirit, Inc.**, which provides hygiene and dignity resources to students. The message of the story reflects a larger movement to make every student feel seen and supported.

If your school or youth group wants to start a dignity drive:

- Collect hygiene essentials like deodorant, toothpaste, soap, and pads.

- Partner with local shelters or school social workers.

- Host a "Day of Dignity" to combine conversation, creativity, and care.

For real-world inspiration, visit:

🌐 **www.spirit-np.info**

(Spirit, Inc. a 501(c)(3) nonprofit working to end hygiene poverty and restore student dignity.)

🧠 2. Mental Health & Confidence Resources

If you or someone you know is struggling with self-image, shame, or anxiety:

- **The Jed Foundation (JED):** www.jedfoundation.org

- Support and resources for student mental health.

- **NAMI (National Alliance on Mental Illness):** www.nami.org

- Free, confidential help for individuals and families.

- **Crisis Text Line:** Text **HELLO** to **741741** (U.S.)

- 24/7 text support from trained volunteers.

Remember: Courage doesn't mean pretending everything's fine.

It means reaching out when it's not.

✍️ 3. Unmask Your Power — Classroom & Youth Projects

Educators and student leaders can use *The Mask Society* to start conversations on:

- Confidence vs. conformity

- Social media pressure

- Hygiene dignity and shame

- Emotional honesty and belonging

Start a truth wall, poetry project, or art showcase.

Encourage students to design their own *"Unmask Your Power"* activities.

To request a **discussion guide**, contact **spiritempowerment21@gmail.com**

💬 4. Join the Ripple

Every movement begins with one person willing to be real.

Keep it going — online and off — using the hashtag **#UnmaskYourPower**.

Share your art, your words, or your story.

Because every time you do, someone else finds their reflection in yours.

A portion of proceeds from this book helps fund hygiene kits through Spirit, Inc.

Together, we're building confidence, compassion, and change — one voice at a time.